SOMETHING HAS TO HAPPEN

MAARTJE WORTEL

TRANSLATION BY / *VERTALING DOOR*
JOZEF VAN DER VOORT

Something Has To Happen
by Maartje Wortel

Translated from the Dutch
by Jozef van der Voort

First published in English
by Strangers Press, Norwich, 2020
(part of UEA Publishing Project)

Distributed
by NBN International

Printed
by Swallowtail Print, Norwich

All rights reserved
© *Maartje Wortel, 2020,*
published by Das Mag Publishers
Translation
© *Jozef van der Voort, 2020,*
mentored by David Doherty

Editorial team
Nathan Hamilton, David Colmer, Michele Hutchison,
Bas Pauw and Victor Schiferli

Editorial assistance
by Senica Maltese, Eirini Maniatopoulou and Tyler Walter

Cover design and typesetting
by Office of Craig

Main body text is set using Arnhem,
Headings are set in Nord

The rights of Maartje Wortel to be identified as the author and Jozef van der Voort to be identified as the translator of this work have been asserted in accordance with the Copyright, Designs and Patents Act, 1988. This booklet is sold subject to the condition that it shall not, by way of trade or otherwise, be lent, resold, hired out, stored in a retrieval system, or otherwise circulated without the publisher's prior consent in any form of binding or cover other than that in which it is published and without a similar condition including this condition being imposed on the subsequent purchaser.

ISBN-13: 978-1911343349

Something Has To Happen

CONTENTS

SOMETHING HAS TO HAPPEN   5

THE CAMP   9

IT'S HAPPENED ALREADY   19

strangers press

SOMETHING HAS TO HAPPEN

The bathroom door doesn't lock any more; it got kicked in during a party. We've never had it fixed. My husband says, Nobody in this family should ever feel embarrassed or unsafe; locked doors are for prisons. He says, This isn't a prison.

Every morning before he goes to work, my husband stands in front of the mirror in his underpants, his belly bulging. He has a hard, rough way of brushing his teeth and three times a week he shaves with a razor he got long ago from his father, one of those old-fashioned things with a gold handle, a brush and all that. I don't know how he can bear to shave after what happened to our son.

My husband says, Objects are innocent by definition. He also says, There's nothing we can do; it was his decision. Things turn out the way they turn out. He says, Think of our daughters, the children we still have, and he also says, I owe it to my own father, for Christ's sake, don't you get that?

He says so many things, but when he talks he looks like gravity weighs more heavily on him than on other people; like he only walks upright against his own better judgement, because you have to walk upright if you want to get anywhere.

I hear him gargling, his bare feet thumping impatiently on the bathroom tiles. He sounds like a horse in a trailer: Get me out of here. I hear the tap running, water and snot and toothpaste pouring down the drain to a place below ground. I sit on the edge of the bed listening to my husband's body, and against everyone's well-intentioned advice I stay out of the bathroom myself. The door remains locked to me. When my husband says, You need to take care of yourself, rituals are the best way to get a handle on life, I say, I could say the same to you, that you need to take care of yourself. You're taking up more and more space, you've got fat. You never used to be like this. *We* never used to be like this.

So what were we like? my husband asks. His tone is harsher than usual.

I shrug, not because I don't think it matters, but because I don't remember. In a quiet voice, I say, Different.

Yes, my husband says. Everything is different now. He sighs and repeats himself. Everything is completely different.

We we eat our breakfast in silence. My husband eats quickly. Eating isn't the only thing he does quickly; it's like he wants to get everything over with as soon as possible. I squash breadcrumbs with my finger.

When my husband leaves for work he says, I'm taking the car today. Sure, I say. But I think, You need to keep moving. You of all people.

He gives me a dry kiss on the lips, walks to the garage, opens the door, gets in the car and starts the engine. When he drives off I think, He's gone now. I also think, Our son used to love strawberry milkshakes. And I realise that something has to happen. I can't spend my whole life thinking about strawberry milkshakes and avoiding the bathroom. I need to start with my husband, he needs to be helped first.

In the utility room, I sort through the laundry. My husband's clothes are ugly and scruffy; you'd never guess from this pile of worn cotton that he used to be slim and stylish. I toss everything into the washing machine and wash it at ninety-five degrees: *whites/colours*. From a stool, I watch the drum spin, the wet clothes clumping on the sides and dropping to the bottom when the drum starts spinning the other way. I think about strawberry milkshakes again. I need to try and forget the strawberry milkshakes. Everyone says the same: Change things up, you need to adjust the way you think.

Once the washing is done, I toss the clothes into the tumble dryer. Then I take them out of the dryer and start again. I repeat the wash and dry cycles until my husband gets home. Ninety-five degrees, then the dryer. I hope he'll notice a change when he gets dressed. I can say, We're in a bad way. Even your biggest clothes don't fit you any more. I'll wait until tomorrow, when he comes out of the bathroom. I'll say, Just look at yourself.

We can cry about it together.

The next day, the morning starts like any other morning. From the bathroom I hear thud, thud; a tap running; the scrape of the sharp razor over his skin. I sit on the bed and wait for him. Something could change today. When my husband comes into the bedroom, he glances at me and picks up his clothes from the bed. He puts them on. I hold my breath.

What? he asks when he sees me looking at him.

Just look at yourself, I say.

My husband looks at himself. I don't see anything, he says.

Your clothes barely fit you, I say.

What are you talking about?

Your clothes have never been so tight on you before.

They fit me just fine, he says.

I can tell he feels rejected though. I need to say something, change the subject, but all I do is watch as he picks his socks up from the floor. I'd been hoping my husband would take the first step, even though he's never been that way. I notice him sucking in his belly as he leaves the room.

Over breakfast, he reads the paper. He looks tired; he mustn't be getting a wink of sleep at night. After fifteen minutes or so he says, I think I'll head off to work early today. He kisses me goodbye.

See you tonight, he says. I won't be late.

I watch him walk to the garage and I want to call him back. I want to say, Don't go today. I want to grab hold of him and say, Stay here. I want him to tell me it'll all be OK, but all my husband will say is, People need to sort out their own problems. You can't force it. Or he'll say, These things take time.

THE CAMP

To be honest, I hadn't really been OK for a long time. Very much not OK, in fact. I'd been fairly secretive about it, but eventually I started telling anyone who would listen I was finding it all pretty tough. Just keeping going. One guy I spoke to suggested I get some therapy.

What kind? I asked. I didn't dare tell him I'd already tried just about everything and my last therapist and I had *both* given up in the end.

The last one was a sweet woman, maybe a little too sweet. The first time I saw her, she said, I'm not a therapist; I'm a treatment provider. I'm going to treat you. She asked, How do you want to be treated?

I looked at the pictures on the wall. They were mainly posters for art exhibitions at the Singer Museum in Laren. This sweet woman must have been running her practice for years now, judging by the posters, but she didn't look all that old. She may even have been attractive. Her hair was pinned up untidily yet elegantly and she was wearing a loose-fitting pink blazer over a delicate white blouse. It didn't look like she had a bra on. Or like she needed one. It might sound as though I was distracted, but my eyes swept across the room in less than a second, I understood where I was and who I had in front of me, and I answered her question almost immediately, a little louder than I'd intended: Like myself.

The sweet woman placed her hands on her lap. They were pale and delicate — almost as delicate as her blouse. It looked a little posed, like she was a newsreader from the days when newsreaders still sat behind desks, and like she was about to read some very bad news to an audience of millions. Her eyes took on a certain glow — beautiful, as if the sun was shining through them, but insane too, like the sunlight was also hellfire.

I've never heard that before, she said. Nobody has ever said that to me before.

Oh, I said. She was looking at me strangely, so I quickly added, These things happen. As if I needed to reassure her. I thought maybe it bothered her that nobody had ever said that to her before. I also wondered whether I was now guilty of something, or if I'd already made a mess of the whole course of therapy with my very first response.

She cleared her throat, recovered herself and spoke in a loud, pure voice. Like yourself, you say. Fine. Let's get to work.

I pictured both of us rolling up our sleeves and knuckling down to a job that might well cost a lot of effort but that we'd make a success of all the same.

For a few months, I talked to the sweet woman every Friday morning. I normally felt fairly good at the start of the week; not amazing but definitely OK, the way most people feel most of the time. But on Fridays, when we finished talking and I left her room, closing the door behind me and stepping out into the fresh air, back into everyday life, I felt exhausted — as if she'd taken something from me. Like I'd left a piece of my heart with her. That's literally how it felt; part of it was still in her room, with the posters from the Singer Museum, lying on her big, gleaming desk. Something she could use to confront her clients (she preferred not to call us patients).

What is this?

Meat, I think. Or so it looks, anyway.

Not quite.

I don't know.

Look closely.

No idea.

Look closer.

Is it... part of a heart?

Exactly. And what do you think when you look at it?

Um. Somebody's dead?

When you see a heart, you think of death. Interesting.

I mean. There must be somebody walking around out there with a hole in their heart, was the first thing I thought. Nobody can live without a whole heart. So I ended up thinking about death.

Indeed. Why didn't you say so out loud? There's somebody walking around out there without a heart. Precisely. And what do you think that means?

Time after time, I was amazed at how my body managed to keep working. Without a functioning heart, I mean. Empty. And yet it kept on going. Until I thought, Soon it'll run out, and then I'll just keel over at the tram stop or in the supermarket. Or even worse, at home.

After a few months of treatment, I decided to share this feeling with the provider — I felt it should be part of the therapeutic conversation — so I told her I had the strong impression she'd taken something from me. The whole idea was that I should tell her exactly what I felt and thought and experienced and saw and went through, after all, but so far we'd only really talked about my childhood, and my childhood self was a different person from who I am now; it was like I'd outgrown myself.

I remember she was wearing a long skirt that covered her knees and a light-blue blouse. Sitting across from her again, I told her I thought she was a very sweet woman. She smiled and said she thought I was a very sweet woman too. We both said thank you.

We looked at each other for a few seconds without saying a word; it was a look of understanding. She was holding her hands in exactly the same way as when we first met during the intake interview. I saw her press her palms together. Small white hands, which themselves had sought out other hands to hold.

I thought I saw her blush. And because I thought she was blushing, I went a little red too. It crept over my entire face.

When I'm in love, I leave myself behind inside the person I'm in love with every time we part. As if I've given up my place. And that's how I feel now. Every time I leave here. This office, I mean. But in a different way.

It feels like you're leaving yourself behind when you leave here? she asked.

Yes, I said.

As if you've given yourself away?

Yes.

She cleared her throat and glanced at one of the posters on the wall behind me, or maybe at nothing in particular, then fixed her bright eyes on mine.

OK, Liseth. That brings us to the next question — and I have to ask you this, do you understand?

I told her I understood.

OK, she said again. Are you in love with me?

I hadn't been expecting that. My mind is always elsewhere when people ask unavoidable questions.

No, I said.

Are you sure?

Yes.

For the record, it's a completely normal phenomenon, you know. People fall in love with each other. Men with women. Women with men. Men with men. Women with women. Clients with treatment providers. It happens all the time.

I had no time at all for a lot of things that happened all the time.

No, I said. That's not it. I just don't want to leave so much of myself behind any more.

You want to be yourself.

I nodded.

Like when you first came here.

What?

You expressed that wish before, she said. In our first session. Maybe that's the problem.

The problem? I asked.

That you're asking that of me.

I'm not asking anything of you, I said.

Yes, you are. You're absolutely certain you aren't in love with me? she asked.

No. I mean, yes.

The treatment provider didn't reply. She waited.

I dream about you sometimes, I said.

Dreams don't mean anything.

Don't you want to know what I've been dreaming?

No. I'm interested in the facts.

I've never been in love with you.

But it feels like I'm taking something from you? You have the same feeling with me as when you're in love with someone?

I think so. But it's my own fault. I think I have to give you something, so I do. And then I have second thoughts. I want to come and take it back again. But I can't. So I don't think that this is working.

That what's working?

This. It isn't working. Not this way, I said. It won't work like this. It doesn't help, all the talking. I've tried so many therapists, but I never really feel OK. It never gets better.

You want to give up? she asked me.

I nodded. And for a brief while, I really did give up. But nobody can keep that up for long.

Now we're pretty much back where we started. I was saying someone suggested a particular type of therapy.

What kind? I asked.

The man I was talking to explained how he knew this other man who'd got a lot out of a lumberjack camp for men. You didn't have to talk all the time. You were outdoors. You chopped wood. You made fire. You were among men. And if you wanted to, you could scream at the trees. If you didn't want to, then you didn't have to. You didn't have to do anything. You just had to turn up, once you'd registered and ticked a week on the form.

But I'm a woman, I said.

That doesn't have to be a problem, he said. He was an acquaintance I'd bumped into at a party where I didn't know anybody else.

So I called up the organiser of the lumberjack camps. I told him my name was Liseth.

Liseth? the organiser asked.

I heard him repeat my name, and, for a brief moment, it felt like I'd never come so close to the truth before. I mean: I called the man up. I said my name. The man repeated my name. And then I was back to myself. The ball was in my court.

Yes, I said.

And you're calling for...?

I'm calling for me.

I won't go through the whole conversation here. Long story short: at first the organiser thought it was a fairly insurmountable problem that I wasn't a man, but, after we spent some time talking, he said, Maybe these things aren't so clear cut. If you don't have a problem peeing outdoors, then you can register for our camp.

No problem, I said. With the peeing. No problem at all.

The camp started at five on a Friday afternoon. The participants all received a route map in advance in a big brown envelope sealed with an alarming amount of sticky tape. There was an Opinel knife in there too. It felt like a vaguely perilous treasure hunt — like our whole lives were leading up to this moment.

I used to strip branches with my father's Opinel, sharpening them to a point so I had my own weapon. I would take the branch to bed with me at night, not only to defend myself against intruders, but also to stroke the wood, which felt so smooth once I'd removed all the bark. So soft, even though you could kill someone with it.

I was once left out in the woods near Lage Vuursche with a bunch of classmates when I was little. I remember thinking it was a joke at first, that they wouldn't leave a busload of sleepy and disoriented primary schoolchildren on their own in a deserted forest and just tell them to figure it out, but that sort of thing was clearly still allowed back then. After an hour of messing about, shouting, screaming, playing stupid pranks and pulling silly faces with torches under our chins, we realised we really did have to find our own way home. But we weren't afraid. We just started walking. I remember feeling properly grown up for the first time in my life as I finally walked down our street at sunrise and saw my house.

At home, we used to play charades to stave off boredom during long winter evenings. We didn't play in teams or for points; my family isn't competitive that way. We just took turns acting things out for the others to guess. It was my turn to act out an occupation. I stood up from the leather pouffe with the idea that I was a lumberjack, and as I took my place, an axe materialised in my hand, a trucker's cap appeared on my head and my muscles started to grow, straining against my blouse. I became a man. I was in the forest and I started chopping wood.

Lumberjack, said my father, mother and brother instantly.

For a moment, I glowed with pride at the fact they'd got it so quickly. But, at the same time, I felt caught out. They weren't supposed to guess straightaway, as there'd be nothing left of the game.

So I told them I wasn't a lumberjack. Nobody believed me, but I insisted.

They continued guessing for a good ten minutes while I went on chopping down tree after tree, splitting logs to get me through the rest of the winter.

My brother sighed impatiently the whole time. After a while, he said, You definitely are a lumberjack, though. Or you're an idiot waving her arms around and pretending to be a lumberjack. I don't know what else you could possibly be.

I knew I had to come clean. But I didn't want to admit defeat fully, so I said, Yes, but I'm not just any old lumberjack.

Oh no? my father asked.

No.

What kind of lumberjack are you then?

I couldn't explain. I knew, but there was no way to put it into words.

By the time I parked my car in front of the solitary house surrounded by fir trees, a few of the men had arrived already. The ground was soft with pine needles, moss, insects, something alive. It felt springy under my feet. The air went deep into my lungs. It woke me up.

The men were standing outside the house drinking tea from big mugs. They looked sweet, all holding their mugs, making small talk in the middle of the forest. I'd somehow been expecting bottles of beer. I guess that says more about my idea of men than it does about the camp. That said, alcohol wasn't allowed this week. The brochure explained how we weren't here to find simple ways to complicate our issues.

The men looked at me, unsure how to approach me — as a woman taking part in a men's camp, or as one of them.

The camp leader said, This is Liseth.

I recognised his voice from the phone.

She's one of us this week.

They seemed to accept that easily enough. It bothered me a little that he implied it was only for the one week, but I didn't say anything.

We'd all paid a lot of money for a week in a forest where nobody would ask anything of us. The arrangement for most of it would be that you could talk whenever you wanted. In practice, that meant most of the participants said nothing. During the day we wandered through the forest looking for wood and in the evenings we used it to build two fires. One fire to keep us warm, one for the sausages and burgers. I heard the usual bad jokes while we were cooking, like,

You let us handle the meat, or, Here's a tasty sausage for you. But it wasn't too bad beyond that.

Sexism is all in your mind, said one of the men.

Everything is all in your mind, said another.

I'm adapting to you lot this week, I said. You aren't adapting to me. That isn't all in my mind, is it?

This is a men's camp, said the coach. That's how it is. You knew what you were getting into.

Yes, I said quietly. But I was still grateful to the pioneering women who had gone before me, over the centuries.

We were each assigned a tree in the forest to scream at. The coach tapped a tree and then pointed at one of the participants, like how the P.E. teacher used to pair students up to prevent bullying, and we ended up standing in a sort of circle, fairly close together

We weren't meant to attack the tree physically; instead, we had to resolve things with words. The men started screaming, without exception. When one of them screamed louder, another would outdo him. Anyone strolling through the forest would have thought there was a brutal massacre going on and called the police, to be on the safe side. They would have turned up, blue lights flashing, to find a bunch of men screaming at trees for no apparent reason.

Stop, the coach called suddenly. Listen to that. The silence. Take a moment to appreciate it.

We stood in front of our trees, listening to the sounds of the forest, to our own breathing, to the occasional cough from one of the others. A few were out of breath from all the screaming. They'd really given it their all.

And *go!* said the coach.

Everyone started screaming at their trees again. Only I didn't do anything. I looked at the bark on the tree, at the ants crawling up and down it, and I listened to the others, the echoes they sent through the forest. Their deep voices carried a huge distance. They weren't really screaming anything in particular, though one of them was screaming what sounded like the names of his family; mostly they just screamed Aaaaaah, aaaaah, aaaaargh! until they were red in the face. All the same, it left me speechless. It sounded magnificent. Like something being released; like a secret.

Don't you want to?

It was the coach's voice.

No, I said.

It might seem scary, but —

It isn't scary. This is what I want. To stand here by this tree.

Listening to the others. Listening to the echo. How everything always comes back to you. Is that OK?

Yeah, of course, said the coach. Great, great.

I was hoping he would say no, if I'm honest. No, that isn't OK. You've got stuff to let go of too. You have to scream. Even you.

But the coach knew how the world worked. He believed in The Circle of Life. Where one thing always feeds into another.

On the last night of the week there was a new activity planned: *sitting in the dark.*

When I was sixteen, I went to a summer camp on the island of Texel. There was a boy I was too nervous to dance with. He didn't want to dance anyway. He asked if we could sit in the cloakroom together. We sat there in the dark, surrounded by coats, and drank coke. The coats smelled of the sea.

We're sitting by the sea, the boy said.

The North Sea?

Whatever sea you want, said the boy.

I wanted the North Sea.

After that, I stopped putting the people I met into categories like beautiful or ugly, friendly or unfriendly. Now I think, Is this someone I'd want to sit with in the dark, by the sea?

My next-door neighbour is a Jewish woman who survived the war. She said, If you want to sit in the dark with somebody, it means they're a good person. Everyone else is bad. She said, I know it the moment I set eyes on somebody. Traitor or not. Yes or no.

Maybe sometimes you might want to know more about someone who's bad, I said.

Yes, said my neighbour.

And maybe sometimes you might think someone who's bad can still become good?

Yes, my neighbour said again. That's the kind of thing you think when you're young.

Not long after the liberation, my neighbour had been on the tram in Amsterdam. It was busy and hot. She'd taken off her jumper; people could see the number on her arm. Hey, a blonde woman had yelled through the tram. Look at her, she's got a number tattooed on her arm.

It's my phone number, my neighbour had said quickly.

When she'd got home, she'd felt ashamed of her reply. Why hadn't she just told the truth? Why don't people just tell the truth?
She'd decided to call the number on her arm. Turned out it was the number for the Amsterdam Central Library.

Once, in the new Central Library, I met a man by the magazine racks who asked for my number. I gave it to him; I thought maybe we could talk. We never talked. He spent years intruding on my life by sending me crude text messages. Mostly in the middle of the night. It was at night that he thought of me and at night that he disturbed my rhythm, my thoughts, my mood and my dreams, until eventually I changed my number.

Different things go on at night than during the day. There's no way of knowing what sort of things they are.

Only one of the men volunteered for *sitting in the dark*. We could choose if we wanted to sit indoors in a dark room or outside. I wanted to go outside. It was a little less dark out there and I didn't know if I could trust him. We sat against the back wall of the house.

You need to look at me when you speak, the man said. I'm pretty deaf.

All this time and I hadn't even noticed.

I haven't always been. I can still hear sounds because they're all stored in my brain. People think it must be quiet in your head if you're deaf. But it's never quiet.

I nodded and wondered if it made a sound he could hear.

What can you hear right now? I asked.

I can hear you talking, he said. He pointed at my lips.

You can see me talking, more than anything, I said.

It's the same thing, said the man.

He told me most people look at each other's eyes when they talk. But he didn't. He had to look at lips, at the movements of the mouth, if he wanted to hear people and understand them.

And yet eyes —

Seem to say so much, said the man.

That startled me — the fact that he'd been able to follow me, and also that he could finish my sentence.

I only know if I find someone attractive when I look at their eyes, I said. Don't you miss that?

You mean, do I still find people attractive?

He didn't take his eyes off my mouth.

I don't like looking at other people's eyes. And I don't like it when other people look at mine either.

I feel the same way about my mouth, I said. I think mouths are gross.

We could look into the darkness instead, said the man. Just sit here, in the dark.

OK, I said.

I thought about the treatment provider, the sweet woman. How I'd left my heart with her. I could say whatever I wanted to this man right now, as if he was a tree. He didn't say anything. We just sat there. The silence fed into something else, it surrounded us, but it was inside us too. Like an echo of something you can't hear.

You know what, I said after a while. And then, in a louder voice, I'm not just any old lumberjack. I stood up and the man looked up and then I started screaming as loud as I could, like how the others had stood and screamed. I screamed at the man, at the animals, at the night, at myself.

I'm not just any old lumberjack! I'm not just any old lumberjack! I'm not! I screamed for a good ten minutes, long enough for the other men in the house to come outside and watch me in silence and understand that I wasn't a lumberjack, not just any old lumberjack. I was myself; one, and insane.

IT'S HAPPENED ALREADY

It's your dad. Sorry I keep calling you, but it's good to hear your voice, to hear you say your own name. I know I was never much of a talker with you; all the same, it's what I want now. Maybe you aren't in the mood to listen to me, but there are some things you need to know. I've been trying to remember what I would tell you if you were here. And then I realised: if you were sitting beside me right now, I probably wouldn't tell you anything at all, like how things have been between your mum and me ever since you... well, ever since what you did. I want to, but I can't. As soon as I see her, I clam up because I don't want to make it worse. I never used to be like that with her, but with you I've never really had the knack. If you were here, I'd ask you how your day was. You'd say, Good. And I'd say, Great. I'd think it was a shame you didn't tell me anything else about your life, no matter how small, and that you didn't ask me how I was doing so we could have a conversation. But I wouldn't say anything, because I'd think — no, I wouldn't just think, I'd be adamant people shouldn't ask anything of each other. I regret it now. That I never asked anything of you. That we never sat down together and started talking. Like how I've started talking now without quite knowing where to start. I should have done it sooner. I thought it was better to leave you be. Do you know that feeling? When you know something has to change and you think, Never mind? Or when you have a chance to change things and then forget why you ever thought they should be different? You think, It'll come in time. It'll all come in good time. I was living like everything was yet to happen, but now it's happened already. I'm sorry for calling you, but I need to talk. I never would have believed it of myself either. I went to get help. You might laugh at this, but it was the only way. I went to a medium. One of my crewmates gave me her number. It was the end of the shift and he came over and said, You bottle things up, like me, but here's the number for a woman who won't let that put her off. He gave me a thumbs-up, as if everything was going to be OK. I don't really bottle things up, I just like peace and quiet, but in the end I dialled the number because of the thumbs-up. I felt quite nervous about visiting the medium. I was scared of what she might tell me, and even more scared of what she might not tell me. She opened the door and it looked like she'd been working out. She was wearing jogging bottoms and a vest top, her face was shiny with sweat. She didn't even have any shoes or socks on. Her nail varnish was messy, like how your sisters used to paint their nails when they were little. The woman told me to come with her. I wondered if the session had already started at the front door as

I felt a bit lightheaded. I followed her up the stairs to her little room. There were porcelain dolphins everywhere and a dream catcher hanging by the window. I hoped she wasn't going to ask me about my dreams. There was a sun painted on the ceiling too. This is pointless, I thought. You know what I mean? All that symbolism. But I had to try. We sat down on office chairs at a round table. To start with, the medium got me to pick a card from a deck with yet more dolphins on the back. The card I pulled out said: DON'T THINK ABOUT THE END OF LOVE. LOVE WITHOUT JUDGEMENT.

The medium asked, Have you read the sentence? I nodded, but I thought, There are actually two sentences. Two very different sentences. I wondered if love isn't a judgement by definition. The medium said, Good. Don't forget what you've read. She said, Keep it with you. Then she took the card from my hand and tucked it back into the deck.

The medium said, I think you're someone who prefers breadth to depth, and she waved her arms around like she was swimming breaststroke. She also said, There's an issue with sex. She asked, Do you engage in sex because you have a death wish? Sorry for bringing this kind of thing up, but it's what she asked me. I want to tell you what it was like; I appreciate this must be the last thing you want to know about me and your mum, but let me go on. So she asked me that and I said no. The sex I have with my wife is negligible. We've more or less... It's difficult...

I see, said the medium.

I came here because of my son, I said.

Your son? she asked.

I didn't dare say your wish out loud. I thought the medium would know what I meant because she was a medium, but she said, If there's an issue with your son then he should come and see me himself. I nodded and I couldn't help but laugh. I hoped it was you who'd made her say it and this was the message she had to convey on your behalf, even if it was just to make me laugh and to show me I had no control over the situation any more, that I'd never had any control. That you really did have to go about everything in life yourself and in the end it wasn't my responsibility, much as I'd wanted it to be. Of course I knew there wasn't any other meaning behind the medium's words; she meant what she said. If there's an issue with you then you need to bring it up with her yourself. That's not something you ever did; you never brought anything up on your own. Or did I not see it? People look at me too and think there's nothing going on in my head. Maybe you thought the same. They think people with certain jobs are incapable of thinking.

Dredge operators. Nobody ever stops to consider that you might choose something like that for yourself. The water, a boat. And I've never stopped to consider your choice either; I'd forgotten you also had thoughts of your own that were unknown to me and your mum and your sisters. Maybe even unknown to you. I wish I'd noticed it sooner, spent a little less time looking at myself.

I stayed with the medium for nearly an hour, all told. We talked. She didn't say much worth remembering, but it helped me anyway. Sitting down and talking. Since the medium didn't bring it up on her own, I eventually told her what had happened. I told her about the party, the bathroom. I told her what you did to yourself. What you did to us, really, as I assume it doesn't bother you any more. Does it? I hope not, anyway. I also told her I'd called her in hope of making contact with you, because I knew something had to happen. That it couldn't go on this way. Not like this.

Often, a person exists because we share something with them, said the medium. And if I remember rightly, she also said that when somebody goes away, we stop sharing and so the person ceases to exist, as if they're slowly being erased.

You can keep him alive by seeking out his presence within yourself. You can call him up.

For a moment I thought she was provoking me, trying to make me angry. I'd been hoping we could call you up in a different way and you might appear in that attic room of hers to tell me the whole story at last. But I've realised I can't leave it up to you again, that your side of the story will remain blank and from now on it's my version that counts. So hello, son. This is your father. I hope you can hear me.

Ben is driving over the speed limit. It doesn't bother anybody at this time of day; the roads are quiet, the great exodus hasn't started. Most people are still eating breakfast, reading the paper or lying in bed, gliding their fingers over their phones or their lovers; a kettle whistles, chocolate sprinkles tumble on to the kitchen tiles, a knife glides through the butter, the coffee's run out, curtains slide open or stay closed, computers start up, alarm clocks go off, fitness fanatics and people with resolutions run through the park, apples are peeled, packets of muesli emptied into bowls, tyres pumped up, citrus fruits squeezed, dogs let out, chickens fed, doctor's appointments attended. Day after day. So many people get up day after day. At the same time. Together. And yet alone. Ben has come to hate it, this part of the day. He wants to get it over with as soon as possible, to give it the slip. It's a chore he has to get through, something he too can't escape. The morning will always be there. And that's exactly the problem with the morning; it's like he can't breathe, like the morning is squatting on top of him, fat and insistent, saying, I'll always be here. Come what may.

The others won't be at the dock when he gets there. Nobody will be waiting for him. But these days he likes it that way. Sometimes he arrives just early enough to see a man mopping the floor of the harbourmaster's office. Those people work overnight so no one is bothered by them, so everyone can believe they keep the office clean by themselves. A world without a blemish. Ben puts his foot down on the accelerator. They're used to it, he thinks. We've all got used to it — to the morning, to each other, to this life. The car races along the canal. It's one long, straight road to the village, which starts with a petrol station, followed by the roundabout, the business park, the houses, the centre, and then the exact same monotonous landscape again; the canal, with empty pasture on either side. Some days, he's here even earlier, at dawn. He sees hunters crossing the pasture in the twilight. Always in groups of three. They walk over the field with long strides, awkward and ungainly; they've already shot their quarry. The animals dangle from their necks like garlands. He's never eaten hare before, though he has eaten rabbit. It tasted good, if not quite how he expected. What he's realising more and more often is he's better off expecting nothing. That works sometimes, but not if you know what you're looking for, like the hunters. They know what they're looking for because they know what to expect, because they know what they got out of bed for. That one moment. The sight of the hare. And then the repetition of that one moment. Maybe that's what life is, Ben thinks. One moment. The repetition of that one moment.

He parks the car close to the boat and glances in the rear view mirror. He catches sight of his clean-shaven cheeks. They startle him, and not for the first time. They're almost perfect, so smooth, so unblemished. The father, the son. His crewmates crack jokes about those cheeks; they think it's unnecessary. He laughs along with them, but this is all he has, the only thing he has control over. He takes the key out of the ignition and suddenly feels tired, as though it's only when the day begins that he notices his lost night. He looks at the boat, the excavator arm hanging motionless in the low morning sun. Soon it will scrape over the bottom of the canal again. Day after day, he and his colleagues in their red raincoats haul a hidden world to the surface at the push of a button. The excavator's hand holds bikes, cars, bottles, furniture, bins, diaries, keys, watches, saucepans, tin cans, books, mud. There are people who toss their whole lives into the water. There are even people who toss their animals into the water, or lose them there, as they put it. Ben wonders why he'd been so set on digging things up; why he hadn't become a teacher or an editor after his literature degree. He loved water, loved formless things, and so he'd ended up on the boat. At first people had said, Surely that's not for you. But over time they forgot he was somebody else and stopped asking questions altogether. Even his wife. And maybe he never asked much more of himself or his life either. Yet the depth of the canal and all the junk in it have been making him nervous lately, as if they're dredging up something else altogether.

He fumbles in his trouser pocket and takes out his phone. He looks up his name. Fred. The name they'd chosen for him when he was born, when they still believed in happy endings. No, more: when they'd just assumed there would be a happy ending. Which is what you have to do when you have children, or you'd never have them at all. He glides his fingers over the opening letters of the alphabet: A, B, C, D, E, F. There he is. Fred.

Ben taps the call button and holds the phone to his ear. It goes straight to voicemail, the phone doesn't even ring; it's at home in the kitchen drawer surrounded by bottle openers, scissors, plasters. Ben went through every name in the contact list when he sent out the invitations. He was ashamed at rooting around in his child's private life, it made him feel uncomfortable, but he wanted to make sure everyone had the chance to say goodbye; that they didn't keep anyone at a distance who'd been close to Fred. Ben hadn't found his own name in the contact list. He'd found: Dad. Also: Home. It hit him harder than he could have guessed.

Soon afterwards, Fred's phone battery had run out. They'd waited until the battery was flat and put the phone in the drawer.

This is Fred. I'm not here right now. Leave a message after the beep. Bye.

The first other car of the day arrives at the docks, a man in a boiler suit behind the wheel. He doesn't look at Ben, he looks at his boat, a small cutter. But Ben still feels caught out, as if he's here for a secret meeting. He's had a few secret meetings before, back when the kids were at primary school, with a woman who keeps a yacht moored here. He hadn't even tried to resist; he'd given himself permission. Their encounters had been fleeting and hadn't meant much. It had made him happy, briefly. Afterwards, he decided that was mainly because no one else knew. It was between him and her. He'd realised how unusual it was for him to share something with just one other person in his life. Everything always belonged to everyone.

They would both park their cars at the docks around this time of the morning before approaching one another across the concrete paving. For him, that was the best moment, the way they drew nearer to each other until they were standing face to face. He would wait a second, then glide his finger down her neck and kiss her. There were cameras everywhere, their meetings were almost certainly being filmed. Ben's theory was that nobody would ever look at the footage; there was too much of it. Who would want to look at footage of some deserted docks in the early morning? Who on earth would care? Who would want to wait for two figures to appear onscreen, kiss, and then walk hand-in-hand over to one of their cars, ready to drive off, to leave, heading for who knows where? He'd never intended to leave. That was why he found it easy to stop in the end. It's only now he's standing here and calling Fred that he feels caught out, as if he's only just realised that although he stayed, he's still always done whatever he wanted. He thought that by leading a life of his own, he was automatically doing something for everyone else; that there was nothing for it but to arrange things as he saw fit, as if there was no other option.

Hey, son. It's me again. I still can't sleep. I've never been good at that, but it's getting worse. Because of what happened. I'm aware of it all day and aware of it all night. Sometimes I drift off for a few hours here and there. When I wake up in the night, the first thing I think isn't, What time is it? Or, I fancy some eggs and bacon. I don't try to reconstruct my dreams either. Not any more. I don't look at the gap between the curtains, or at how the sheets have slipped off your mother's hip, or the patch of skin between her knickers and her top. I don't head straight downstairs to fetch the newspaper from the letterbox and read the front page. The first thing I think when I wake up is, Something's wrong. Only to realise a few seconds later that my thoughts are true. Something has gone very wrong. Horribly wrong. Sometimes, during those few hours in the night, I forget what it was. You might be thinking, It's good to forget, Dad. You need to forget. You might think the moments when you can't quite remember what the matter is — the moments when everything goes blank and you're free of your thoughts — that those are the best moments. But they aren't. Not for me. Not any more. My whole body — skin, bone, muscle — constantly feels there's something wrong. The feeling of dread flows through my veins like thick blood, and though it only lasts a few seconds or minutes, that brief interval when I can't tell where the feeling comes from is much worse, so much worse, than knowing what's wrong, however bad it is. Knowing you aren't there any more is easier than feeling an absence and searching frantically within myself, in the moment between sleeping and waking, for where the absence comes from.

    I lie next to your mother, and I look at her. I don't know if she's asleep or just pretending. I don't know how she's doing with that one moment repeating itself in her head, how she's living with her grief. I think your mum has started to look at me very differently. Like I've disappeared for her too. That's partly down to me. I want to touch her, to hold her tight, but every time I think, I might make things worse. I don't want her to think I expect anything from her. I want her to know she's safe. She mustn't feel she has to console me; her own thoughts are enough for her. You know your mother; she's not much of a talker, like you. It gets on her nerves. To her, words only make everything bigger, heavier, more tangible. So I pretend there's nothing much the matter. She doesn't know about the medium; she doesn't know I'm calling you either. I think it would just unsettle her, for no good reason. When I can't sleep at night, I read books. Most of the words don't really get through to me. I read without knowing what I'm reading. And more and more often I think, I'm living without knowing I'm alive. And more and more often I'm unsure if that's because of you, or if you recognised something in me back then — if you were quicker on the uptake. Maybe I should talk to your mum. We should sit down together and look into it all. The things that are different now. Otherwise it'll stop here. And it can't stop here; that can't happen. No way. But there's no point asking you how it's done. How to keep living. This morning, I heard some children playing out in the street. They were kicking a ball against the garage door. I'd thought the new life in those young children would be painful to me, but it wasn't. I couldn't care less about that new life. I don't know what's worse.

He leans against the coffee machine in the deckhouse. He glides his tongue over the roof of his mouth. There are bumps on the tip of his tongue. Vitamin deficiency. He needs to eat better and maybe exercise, get on his bike more. He has enough opportunities. He mustn't let opportunities go to waste. The water slowly bubbles through the coffee and the filter. The machine does what you ask. What did he ask Fred? Not enough. But it isn't his fault. Fred has always been unavailable. There was something about the boy. Ben saw it, but he left it at that. You can't know everything about your child. For a long time, he thought you shouldn't want to know everything either. But now he thinks maybe he didn't know enough.

Things are different with his daughters, who live and study in Utrecht; they just pick up the phone and start telling him how they are. What they think about when they think about Fred. Sometimes it even makes him feel lonely. Nobody ever asks him... No, more than anything, he's never asked enough of himself. Because he thought it would all come in good time, as a matter of course. He'd been counting on a matter of course.

When he finishes his coffee, he walks outside and stands on deck with his hands in his pockets. His coat puffs up in the wind. One of his crewmates hawks and spits into the water. When they pass a fuel station, they moor the boat and Ben hops down on to the embankment. The day is almost done. He needs to buy some liquorice allsorts. Only sweets can pull him out of his thoughts, every now and then.

Hello, son. There's something else I want to tell you. About why your mum and I threw the party. We thought it was better not to explain it to you or your sisters. I barely know anything about my own mother or father, for instance. I mean, I know what I know about them, which is what I saw of them throughout my life. That was enough for me. It was the only way they could stay the mother and father I'd made them into. I wasn't really curious about their story, their life. It might sound harsh, but I was mainly interested in my own life, and I wanted to keep the role my mother and father played intact; they had to stay who they were to me. If I found out more about their personal life, about the time before I existed — what they were like as a boy and a girl, apart and then together; how they felt or what they talked about or what problems they might have had — then it would ruin something for me, or at least I was afraid it would. I thought, what's past is past.

I can still remember how my father put his arm around me one day; it was hot, we were eating ice cream in the back garden, and he took a bite of his ice cream and said he found it so strange that he was the backdrop to my childhood. He said he and I would remember every moment differently, even the ones where we were only eating ice cream. He repeated it: I'm going to be the backdrop to your stories. I felt him give my shoulder a squeeze. I didn't quite understand at the time what he meant about the backdrop. I've never thought about an ending for you, or a backdrop either. But now I can't stop thinking about our backdrop. Yours and mine. The end. And where it went wrong. The kicked-in door. Sometimes I think I didn't show you enough, so you always felt a kind of absence. I've never told you how many girls I've kissed, or why I decided to join the boat, or how I feel when we cast off. I've never told you that I was arrested once, that for a long time I was afraid there was someone hiding under my bed and that my mother and father weren't my real mother and father, that I once almost drowned, or that when I was a child I sometimes got lost because I would often stop and stare at the grass growing between the paving slabs or the hubcap of a car or a spider that had caught a fly in its web and everyone else would keep walking. When I looked up again, I knew I'd been left behind on my own, which added to my fear that I wasn't my mother and father's real child. The moment had come when they'd decided to abandon me, when they didn't want to look after me any more. Usually I felt a hand on my neck soon enough or heard a familiar voice, someone calling my name. I could go with them again. For a little longer. But once I was found by an old man with a limp. He asked me where I came from, and I remember telling him I didn't know. I don't know, I said. And now I'm thinking about the backdrop again, the one my father talked about. The space somebody else comes up with for you. You don't have to feel at home there, you don't have to be OK with it; it just takes a little time to get past it and figure out your own path. For Christ's sake, why didn't you give it a little more time?

 What you didn't know was that the party was supposed to be a new beginning. For a while your mother wasn't sure what she wanted. From herself, from me, from us. She'd been expecting something different from it all. She wanted to tell you and your sisters but I persuaded her not to. I told her she shouldn't scare you with her private doubts; that we were here to show you how easy life can be. No problems in front of the children, I said. I didn't want you to feel rejected. I hoped later in life you would know exactly where you came from when anyone asked. But we've had our problems, your mother and I. To me, problems were a sign of weakness, something for other people. Like floods, wars, rotten teeth, bomb attacks, volcanic eruptions. Suddenly you're part of it; the distinguished company the others talk about. You never escaped it; nobody will ever escape it. But like my father always used to say when we set off on holiday and drove through the countryside: If we're driving, we're driving. If we're driving, it means we haven't got there yet. All I ever wanted was to get there, to reach an end point like I'd always imagined. Like how the boat was an end point for me too. I was on the water and I could take things from there. Your mum and I hadn't quite settled everything, but we'd settled enough. We came up with the idea of a party, a celebration, because we thought happiness could also be a choice, and that choice starts with fun. A party. A fun time. Happiness. And suddenly there's nothing left to choose. What was your backdrop, was our *life*. Still is our life. We don't have much choice, Fred, do you realise that? When you get so ill that you decide you don't want to live any more, when you've tried everything and there's no way out, then you fill in forms, sign on the dotted line and arrange for the doctor to come over one day and give you the drugs. The doctor never comes alone. However weak you are, before you get the drugs, you always have two people asking you if you're sure. They want to hear you say it: Yes, I'm sure. And a second time. Yes, I'm sure. Only then are you allowed to leave. If you can ever be sure about anything. I think I just wish I'd asked you that. Are you sure? I hope so, anyway. I keep trying not to think about the end of love. I'm going home soon. I'm going to see your mother. I'm going to tell her I have no idea what the matter is. That I'll never have a clear picture of what happened. That we might want to know what the matter is, but you can't know everything. That we'll never figure it out. That's the difference between life and death. I'm going to ask your mother if we should try to carry on, if she can ever see me again the way she used to. We don't know where we've come from, but we know where we are. That's what I'm going to tell her. And that we can only hope it's enough. It has to be enough, don't you think?

Ben drives back home. Not too fast, there's traffic. Everyone is heading home. In the village, he stops at the butcher's and asks for a hare. At the off licence he picks up some wine. Potatoes and carrots from the greengrocer. He's going to cook for her. He can't let her leave too. He can't do that to himself, or to her. There has to be someone who chooses happiness. When he gets home, he puts his keys on the table.

He walks over to the fridge and grabs two beers. He's going to call her name; he's going to talk to her when she comes out of her office, when she's done with the daily admin. But first he takes the phone out of the drawer. The charger is missing, but he can use his own. He has the same model. The PIN is straightforward: four zeroes.

He could go through the contact list and find a name he likes the look of; he could call somebody up. A living person. Would Fred's friends have deleted his number already? Or would they see his name on their screen and for a brief moment forget he's dead? It would give them a shock, either way.

Then he gets a shock himself as the messages come pouring in. All voicemail notifications. A flood of unheard messages. He calls the voicemail, puts the phone on loudspeaker and sits down at the kitchen table.

Hi, Fred. It's Dad. I'm calling to say I miss you.

He listens to his own voice, the fractured tone, the wind that sometimes crackles down the line. He hears himself searching for the right words, as if something could still go wrong. He sits there at the kitchen table and listens until he hears footsteps on the stairs, until his wife comes up behind him and puts her hand on his neck. He puts his hand on hers.

nieuw new
dutch **nederlands**
stemmen voices

VERZET is a series of chapbooks showcasing the work of some of the most exciting writers working in Dutch today, published by Strangers Press, part of the UEA Publishing Project.

Each story is beautifully translated and presented as an individual chapbook, with a design inspired by the text in collaboration with The Dutch Foundation for Literature and National Centre for Writing.

1. **RECONSTRUCTION**
   by Karin Amatmoekrim trans. by Sarah Timmer Harvey

2. **THANK YOU FOR BEING WITH US**
   by Thomas Heerma van Voss, trans. by Moshe Gilula

3. **BERGJE**
   by Bregje Hofstede trans. by Alice Tetley-Paul

4. **THE TOURIST BUTCHER**
   by Jamal Ouariachi trans. by Scott Emblen-Jarrett

5. **RESIST! IN DEFENCE OF COMMUNISM**
   by Gustaaf Peek trans. by Brendan Monaghan

6. **THE DANDY**
   by Nina Polak trans. by Emma Rault

7. **SHELTER**
   by Sanneke van Hassel trans. by Danny Guinan

8. **SOMETHING HAS TO HAPPEN**
   by Maartje Wortle trans. by Jozef van der Voort

Supported by

N National Centre for Writing

N ederlands letterenfonds
dutch foundation for literature

This series was made possible by generous funding from The Dutch Foundation for Literature